W9-AZH-523

DATE DUE

DATE DUE
DATE DUE
DATE DUE 03
DATE DUE
11 30 04

Return Material Promptly

Discard

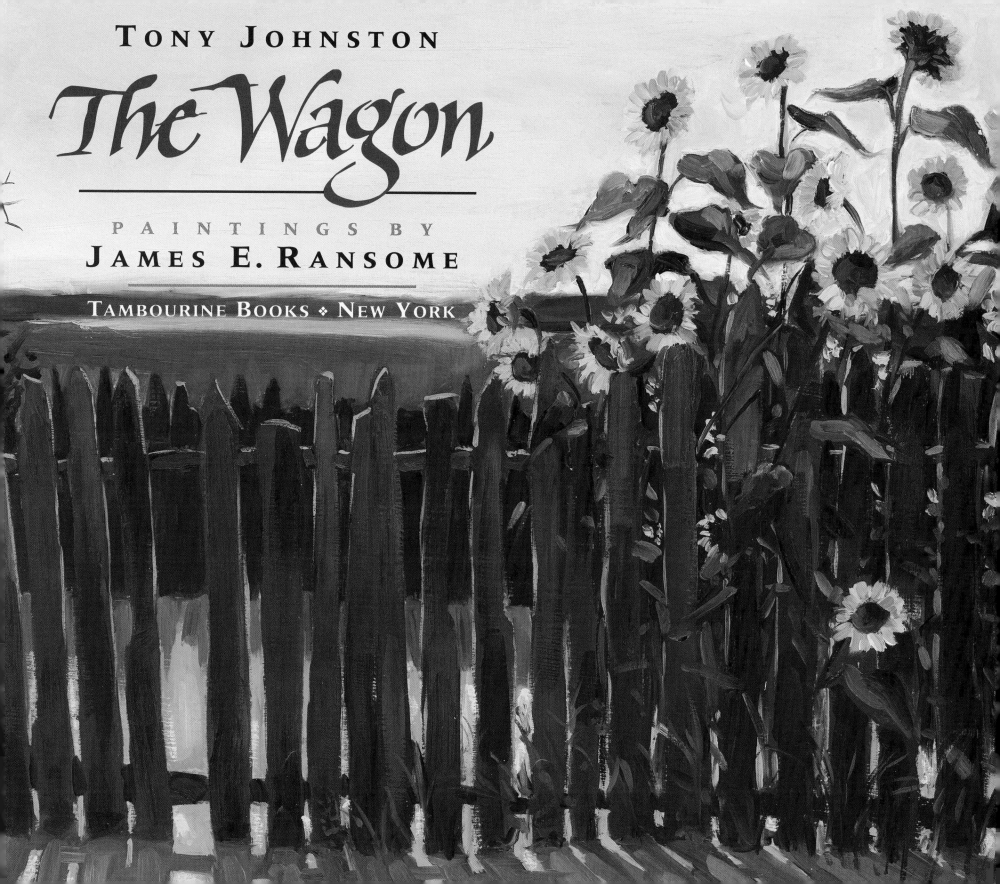

TONY JOHNSTON

The Wagon

PAINTINGS BY
JAMES E. RANSOME

TAMBOURINE BOOKS ✦ NEW YORK

Printed in the United States of America. The text type is Meridien.
The illustrations were painted in oil on paper.

Library of Congress Cataloging in Publication Data
Johnston, Tony, 1942—
The wagon / by Tony Johnston ; paintings by James E. Ransome.—1st ed. p. cm.
Summary: A young boy is sustained by his family as he endures the difficulties of being a slave,
but when he finally gains his freedom, his joy is tempered by the death of President Lincoln.
[1. Slavery—Fiction. 2. Afro-Americans—Fiction.] I. Ransome, James, ill. II. Title.
PZ7.J6478Wag 1996 [E]—dc20 95-53103 CIP AC
ISBN 0-688-13457-2 (trade).—ISBN 0-688-13537-4 (le)

10 9 8 7 6 5 4 3 2 1
First edition

I touch old wood.
   I touch old wounds.   —T.J.

To my second blessing, Maya, with the muffin face
   and big beautiful eyes.   —J.E.R.

One Carolina morning, I was born.
Everything was beautiful that day, Mama said,
especially my skin
like smooth, dark wood.
But like all my family, birth to grave,
my skin made me
a slave.

We lived on a farm, where we worked
for a man.
His house was white as ripe
cotton, the grass green
as spring.
The fields rolled on forever it seemed.
How I hated the place!
I could not go
where I pleased.

My papa was good at building things.
His hands, though huge, made magic
with tools.
Once he built a wagon, like Master
told him.
Though I had lived eight plantings only,
I helped fell a tall oak.
Then I handed Papa his needs
when he called.
"Hammer!" "Saw!" "Nail!" "Awl!"
We built a good wagon
of smooth, dark wood.

Master strolled around it, slow.

Smacked one side. Inspected the wheels

sharp and close, like an auctioneer

checks a horse—

or a slave.

I longed to climb atop that wagon and roll

away.

Master put Papa in charge of it.
Gave us the use of his mules.
In our room, cramped as a cracker box,
my family whooped
at those slave names. We pondered
a change.
At sunup, the mules had been
Robert and James. By sundown, they were
Swing and Low,
from a song we sang about a band of angels
and a better place.
I thought, *Any place is better*
than this,
where all day I heard the whish of the lash,
like the Devil's breath.
When the overseer beat an old man
near to death,
I cried and got whipped,
for that.

Every day now, Papa and I were
allowed
to hitch up Swing and Low and go
for supplies, then come straight back.
No dawdling. No delays.
Or we would be lashed
to the bone.

Sometimes our cargo was slaves,
to be sold.
Sometimes, slaves coming
to the farm.

Papa sang
while the two of us creaked along.
"Swing low, sweet chariot, comin' for to
carry me home."
"What's a chariot?" I asked once.
"Something to bear you off."
"Like this wagon?"
"Like this wagon, but
glorious."
When we had set out, it was just
a wagon. Now it was my glorious chariot.
Maybe some day, it would bear me
away.

Papa was wagon boss. Also in charge of splitting

wood to warm the farm.

Though spindly as a sapling,

dawn to dark, I was to help.

How that rankled me!

I was a *boy*, not a mule.

I longed to do what free

boys do.

I envied all the footloose
things. Even the sun,
and the moon.
At times, I was surprised to feel my teeth
clench up. To feel tears warm
my face.
I brushed them away with a sleeve
and swore, *Tonight I'm going.*
Though I had the grit, I could not quit
my family. So my anger
just kept flowing.
My mama and papa knew.
"Keep courage," they said. "Trust in the Lord."
So I did what I was told.
And I grew.

Stories reached us, like smoke
on the air.
Stories of war.
In some other place, cannons growled.
Soldiers, blue and gray, prowled
other green fields.
I ached to steal away there, to fight
the Slavery Snake.
But I could not go
where I liked.

In spite of war, spring came in a burst
of blooms.
One day, I rested my ax and watched
a bug split its skin and become
a bright, flying jewel.
I wished I could split
my skin too.
I gazed at the wagon, chariot of false
hope.
In rage, I hacked
at its wheels, its spokes.

I got striped good for that.

My grandma bathed my raw back.

"Yours is not the only troubled soul," she said.

"Mr. Lincoln is sometimes overcome

with gloom.

Sees the Country ripped to rags,

as if two furious folks was tugging

at a beautiful quilt.

Sees boys dyin' and dyin'

and dead.

Does he give up?

I hear he chops wood, instead.

Like when he was young. Chopping helps him

go on."

I had a dream.
The President and I, chopping wood
together. By moonlight.
Chopping was easier after that.

As war spread, talk spread,
how the President was torn over the wrong
of slavery. How maybe he would free
all slaves.
Lord, how we prayed.
Then everything changed.
The President wrote some words one day.
We had gone to bed
slaves. But we woke up
free.

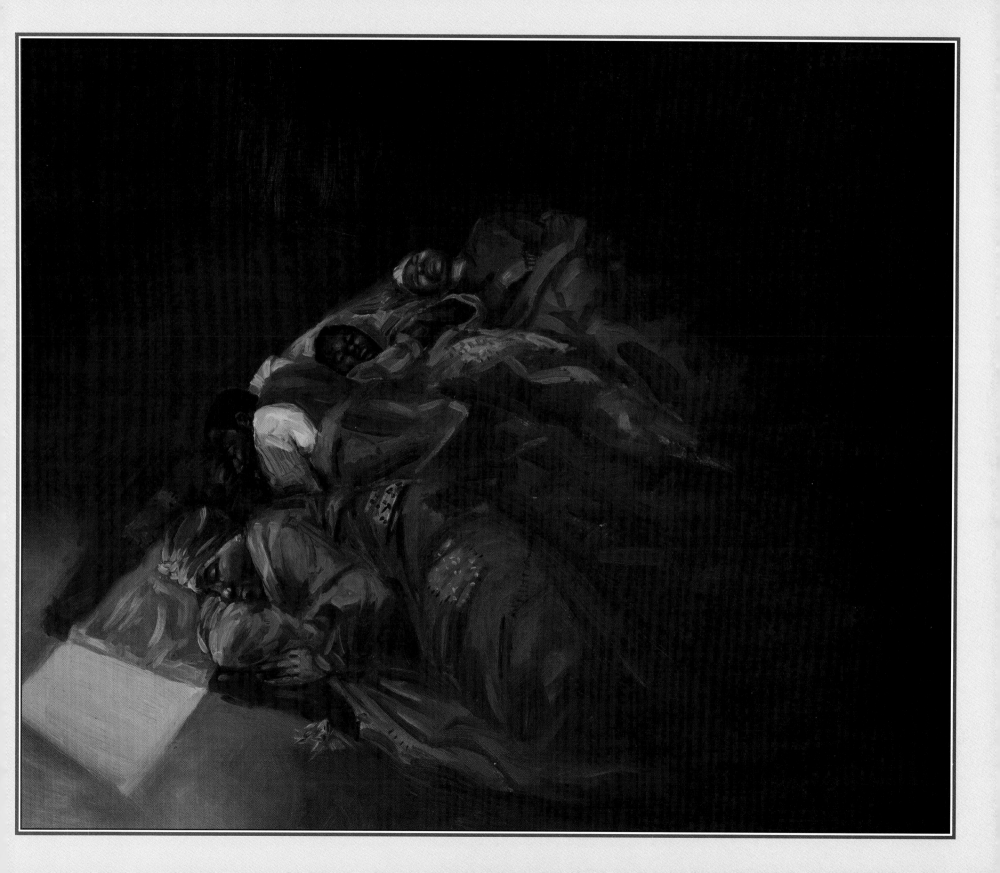

The farm came alive
with song—
one great slave voice, rejoicing
like one great hive a-hum.

I had dreamed of that moment forever,
had done my dance of jubilee
on the sly, stomping
in the wagon, spinning
like a twister, shouting
every song I knew—
a one-boy angel choir.
But when it happened, I wanted
to whisper.
My family held hands in the field
we had worked
and kneeled in the dirt and gave
thanks.

But ol' Freedom dragged her feet,
took her sweet time catching up
to those words.

When at last we left the farm, Master
was sharp-edged, but not mean.
He asked, what did we need.
Papa said, "A wagon."
So that was our farewell, the wagon
we had built long ago. And two mules,
Swing and Low.

It was eerie-quiet as we rolled toward
our new life.
We were scared. Who could see down
Freedom's furrow?
All I could hear was the snuffle
of the mules and the creak of my sweet
chariot.
I looked at my arm,
resting on the wagon flank.
It looked good—my arm
like smooth, dark wood.

Bad news travels fast as
a snakebit wind.
One day bad news blew in.
Just when he could rejoice in war's end,
someone had shot the President
dead.
"Why?" I asked, dazed.
"Don't know," Papa said. "Seems
when you gain something of value, you must
lose something too."

In my life, twelve plantings had come and gone.
I was free. I could go
where I pleased.
I said, "I want to go to the funeral."
So at dawn my family and I set out,
creaking down the road toward
Washington.
Creaking along in a wooden wagon,
to say goodbye to
Mr. Lincoln.